S0-AAC-651

THE TWO BULLIES

Do you know the big statue
called Ni-ou that stands by
the temple gates?

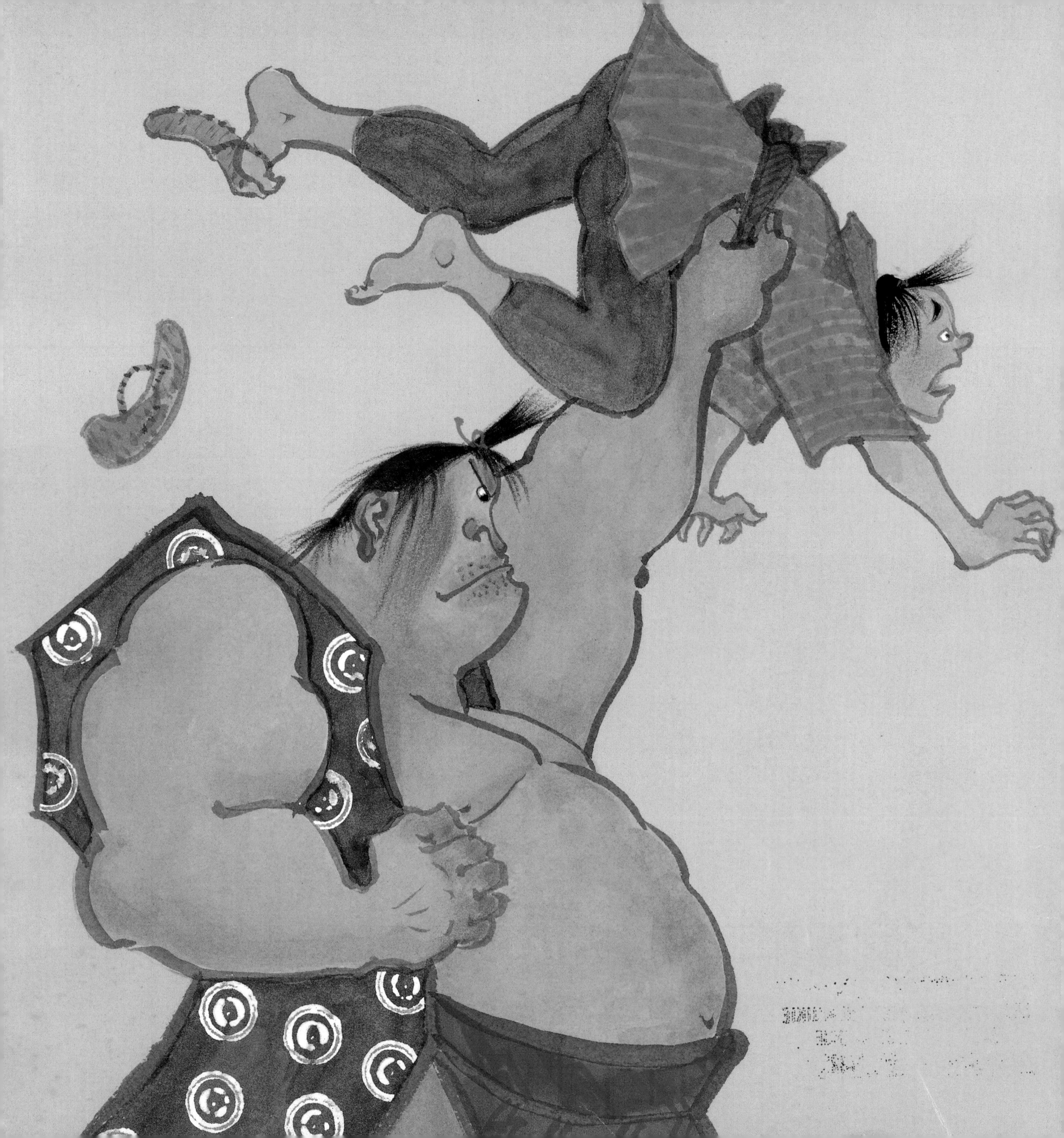

THE TWO BULLIES

JUNKO MORIMOTO

Translated from an original Japanese story by ISAO MORIMOTO

A long time ago, there lived a huge man called Ni-ou. He was so strong that *nobody* could beat him.

So Ni-ou proudly proclaimed himself "the strongest fellow in Japan."

Crown Publishers, Inc., New York

ROWE CHILDREN'S LIBRARY
LEDDING LIBRARY OF MILWAUKIE
10660 S.E. 21ST AVENUE
MILWAUKIE, OR 97222

One day, he heard that in China there was a strong man called Dokkoi.

Ni-ou thought he would challenge him. So he started preparing for the trip, and visited the temple of Hachiman nearby to pray for victory.

As he walked home, a priest suddenly appeared from nowhere.

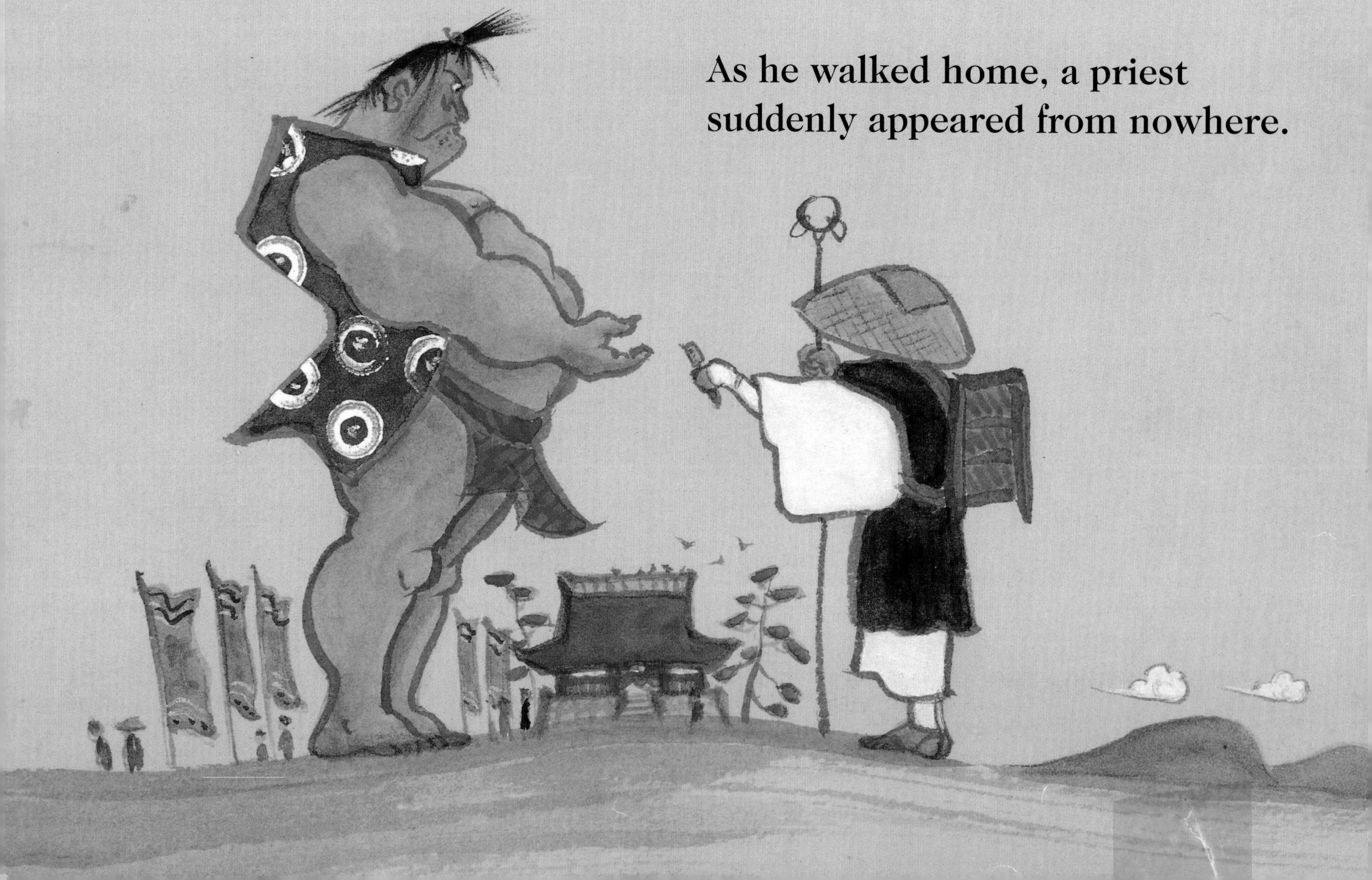

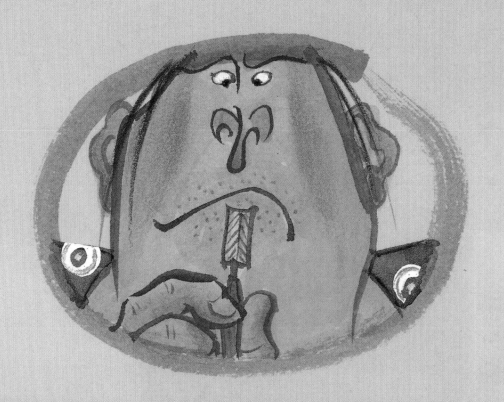

Ni-ou had never met him before, but the priest gave him a file and said that it would cut anything.

"It might come in handy. Take it with you," he said.

"Thank you," said Ni-ou, "but who are you?" And before he had finished speaking, the priest had disappeared.

Ni-ou did not know, but the priest was Hachiman himself.

After rowing his boat for many days, Ni-ou finally crossed the vast ocean and reached China.

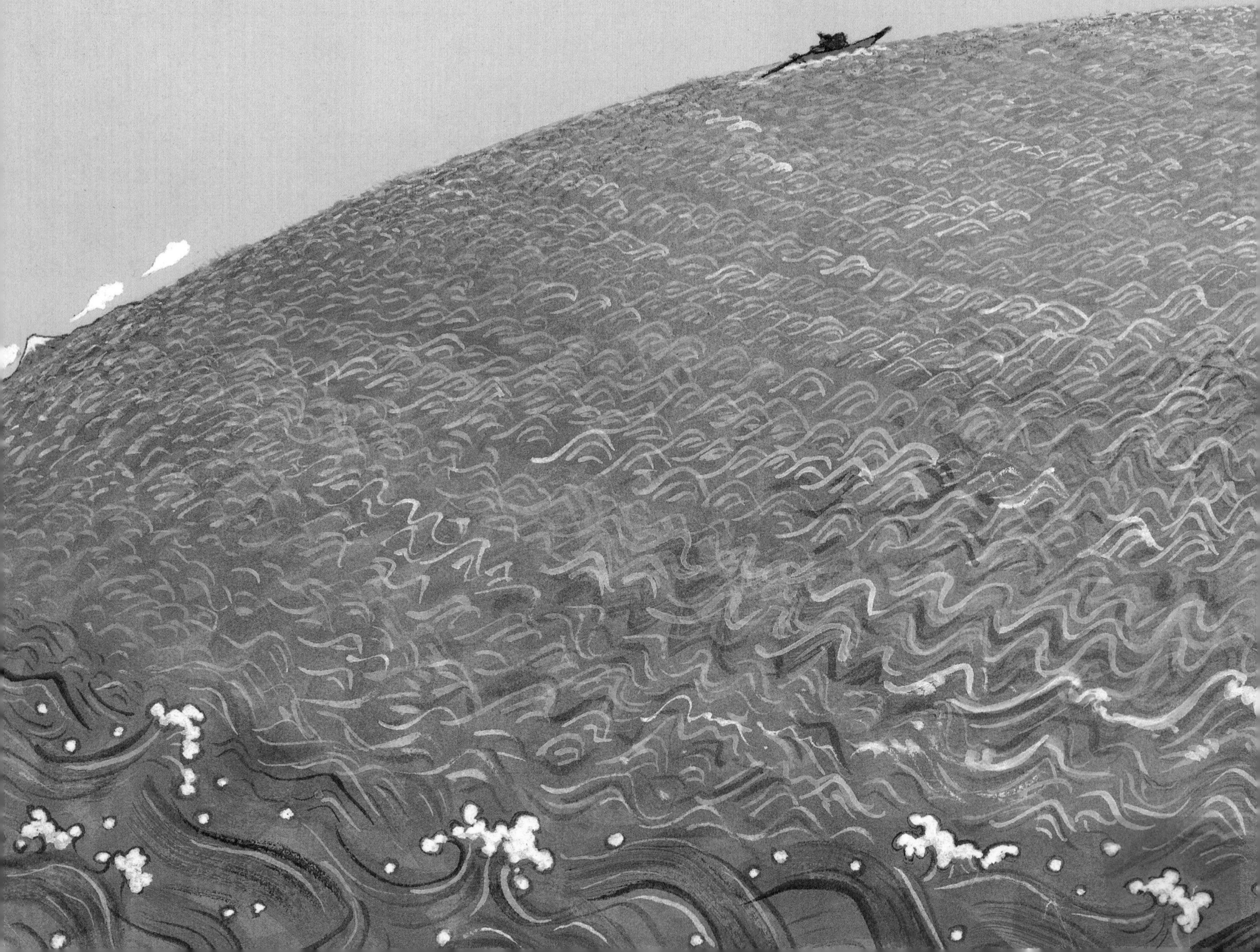

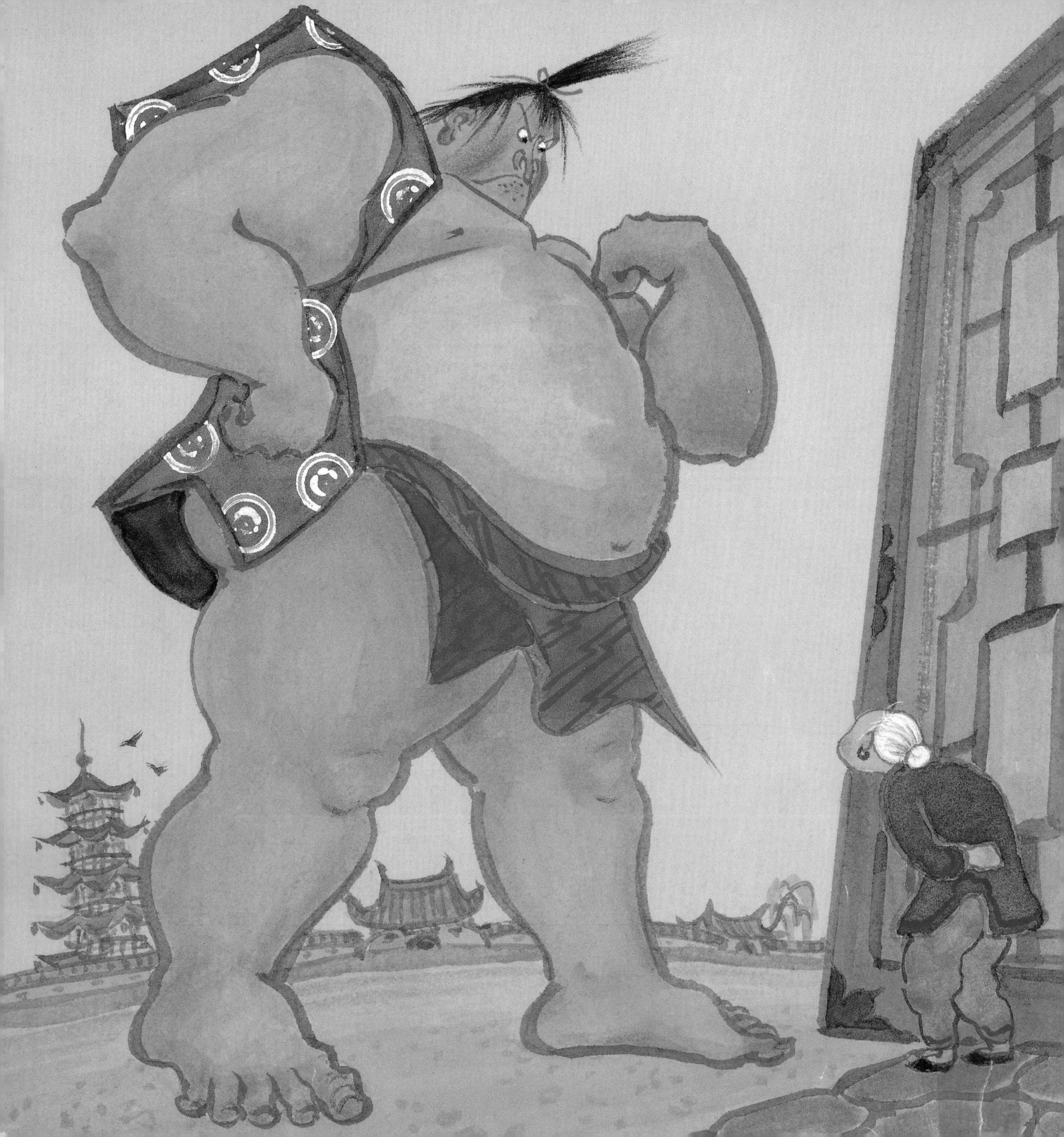

He arrived at Dokkoi's house.

"I am Ni-ou," he shouted. "More powerful than anyone in Japan. I've come to see who is stronger: you or me. Come out and take the challenge!"

But it was a small old woman who opened the door.

"Dokkoi is not at home, but he will be here soon. Why don't you wait for a while?" she said.

So Ni-ou went inside and waited.
And waited. Then...

ZuSHIINNN MIRIMIRI...
ZuSHIINNN MIRIMIRI...

It sounded like an earthquake
in the distance!

"Old lady, what is that sound?"
Ni-ou asked.

"That is the sound of Dokkoi's
footsteps. When he is coming
home, I hear him from miles
away."

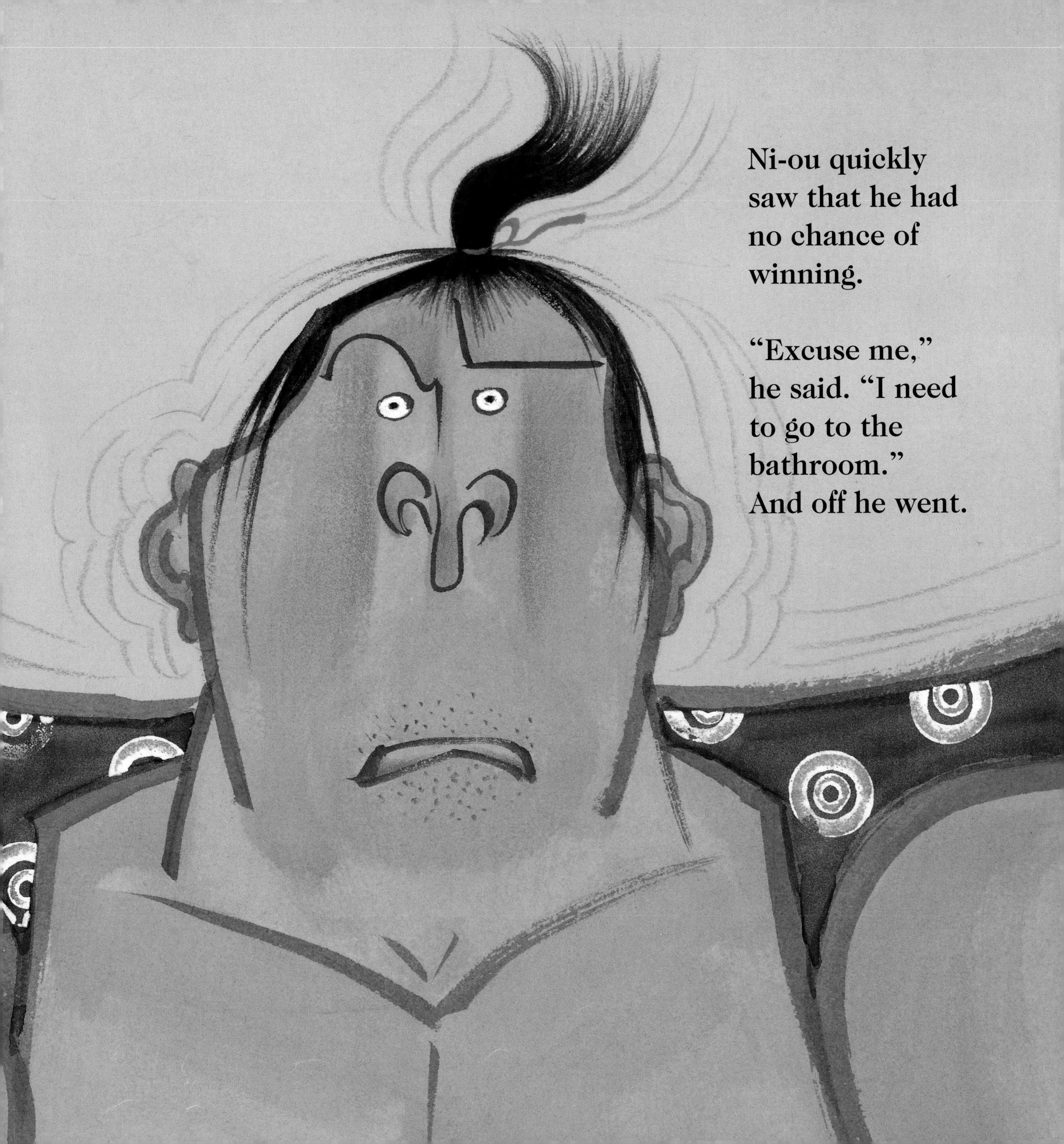

Ni-ou quickly saw that he had no chance of winning.

"Excuse me," he said. "I need to go to the bathroom." And off he went.

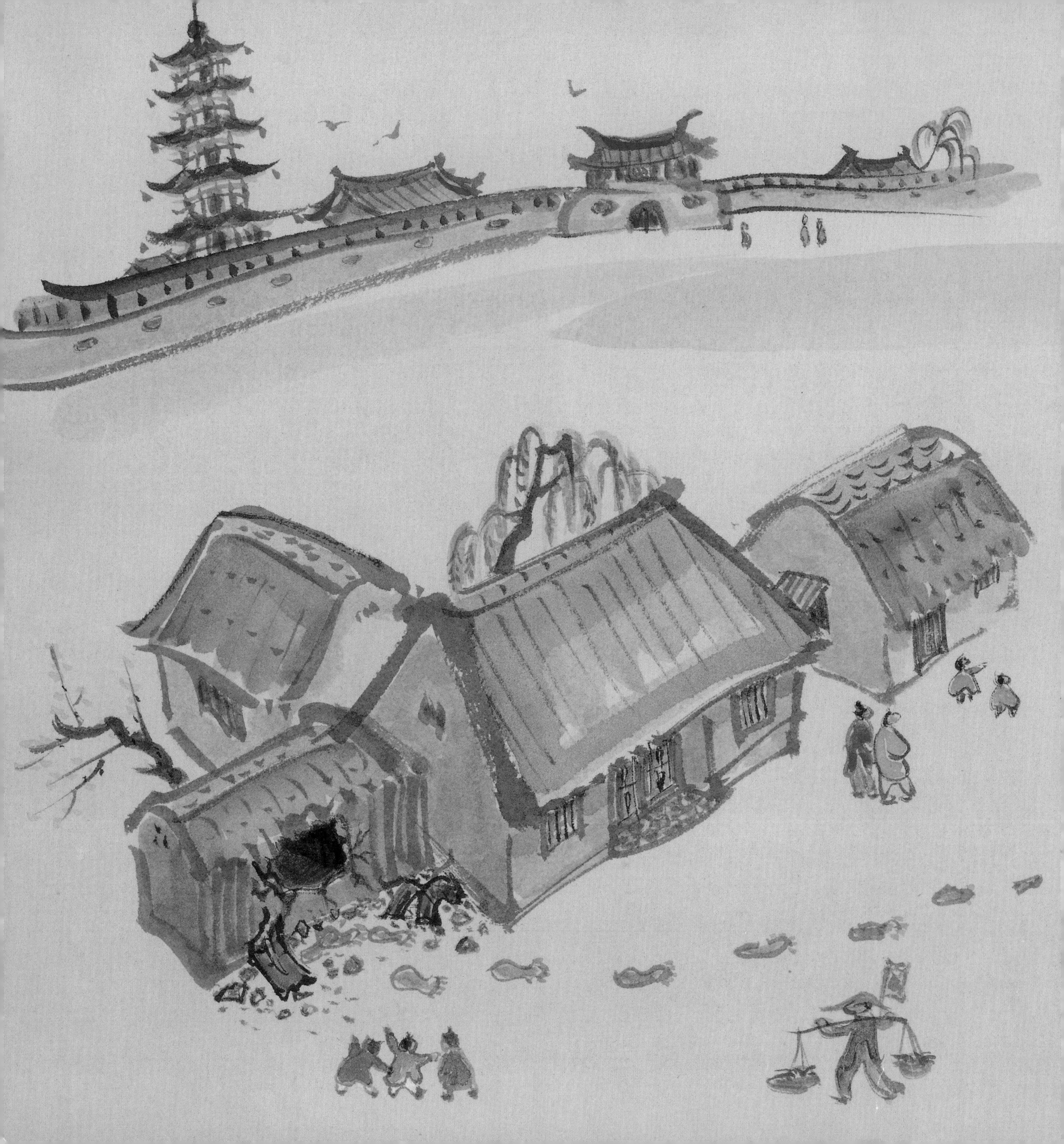

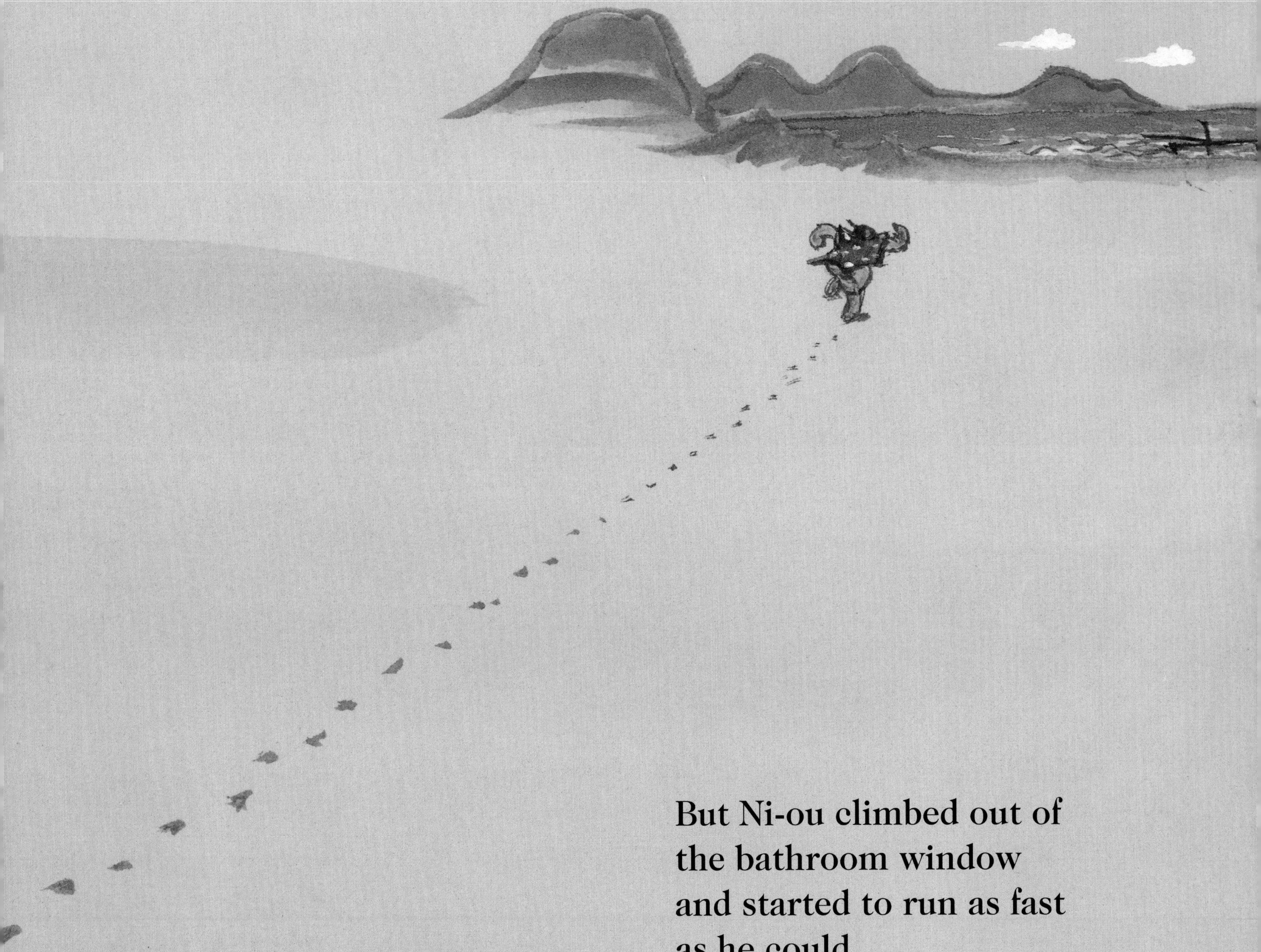

But Ni-ou climbed out of the bathroom window and started to run as fast as he could.

He jumped into the boat and rowed for Japan as if his life depended on it.

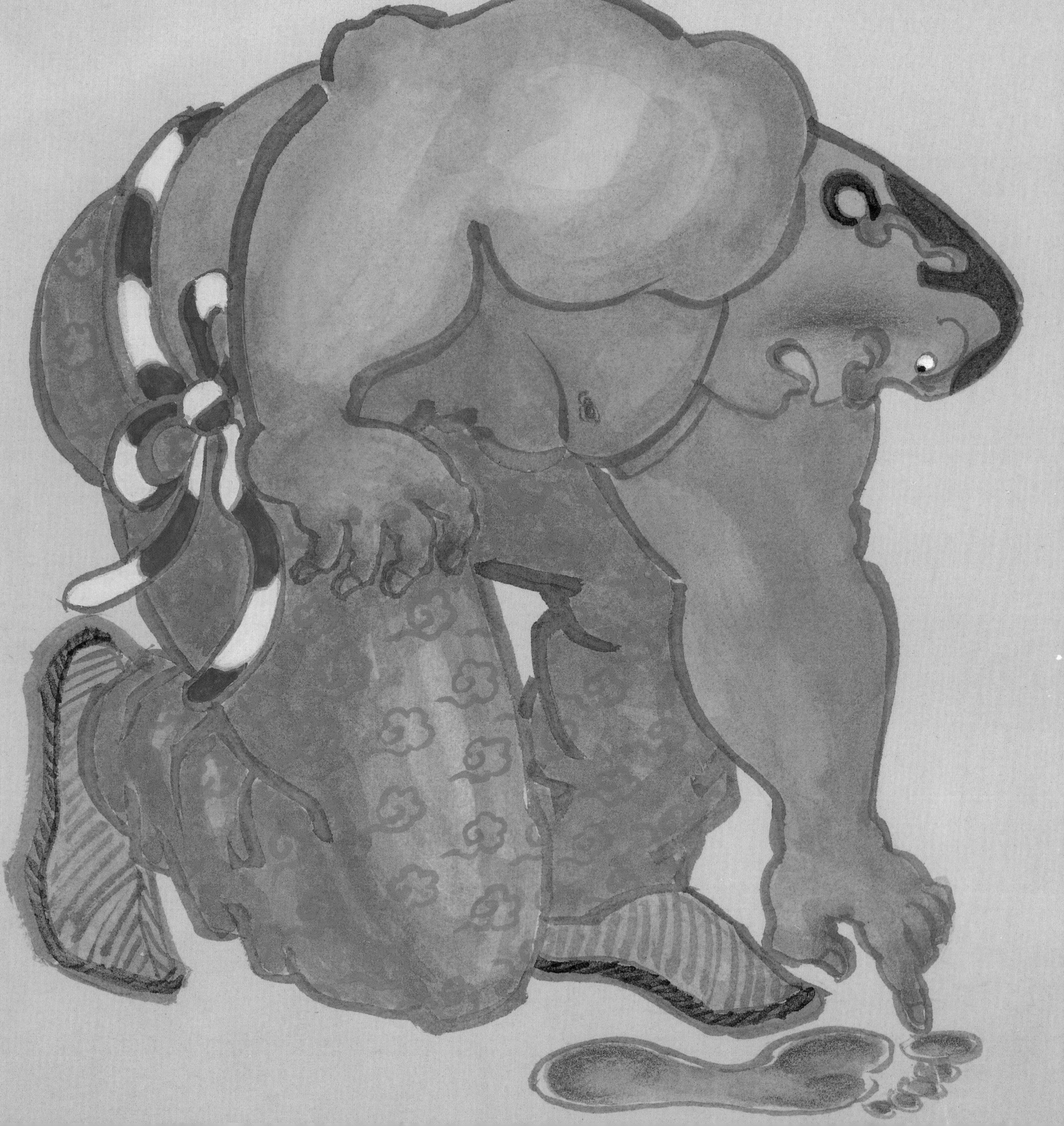

When Dokkoi arrived home, he noticed an enormous footprint.

"Who has been visiting you?" he asked the old woman.

"Shh, he's in the bathroom," she whispered.

Dokkoi looked at the footprint. There was only one man with feet like that: the Japanese giant Ni-ou.

So Dokkoi waited for him to come out of the bathroom.

But Ni-ou didn't come.

Finally, tired of waiting, Dokkoi opened the bathroom door. The bathroom was empty. Ni-ou had gone.

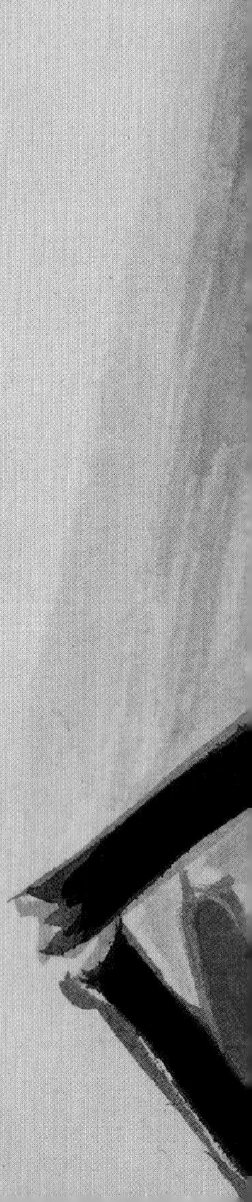

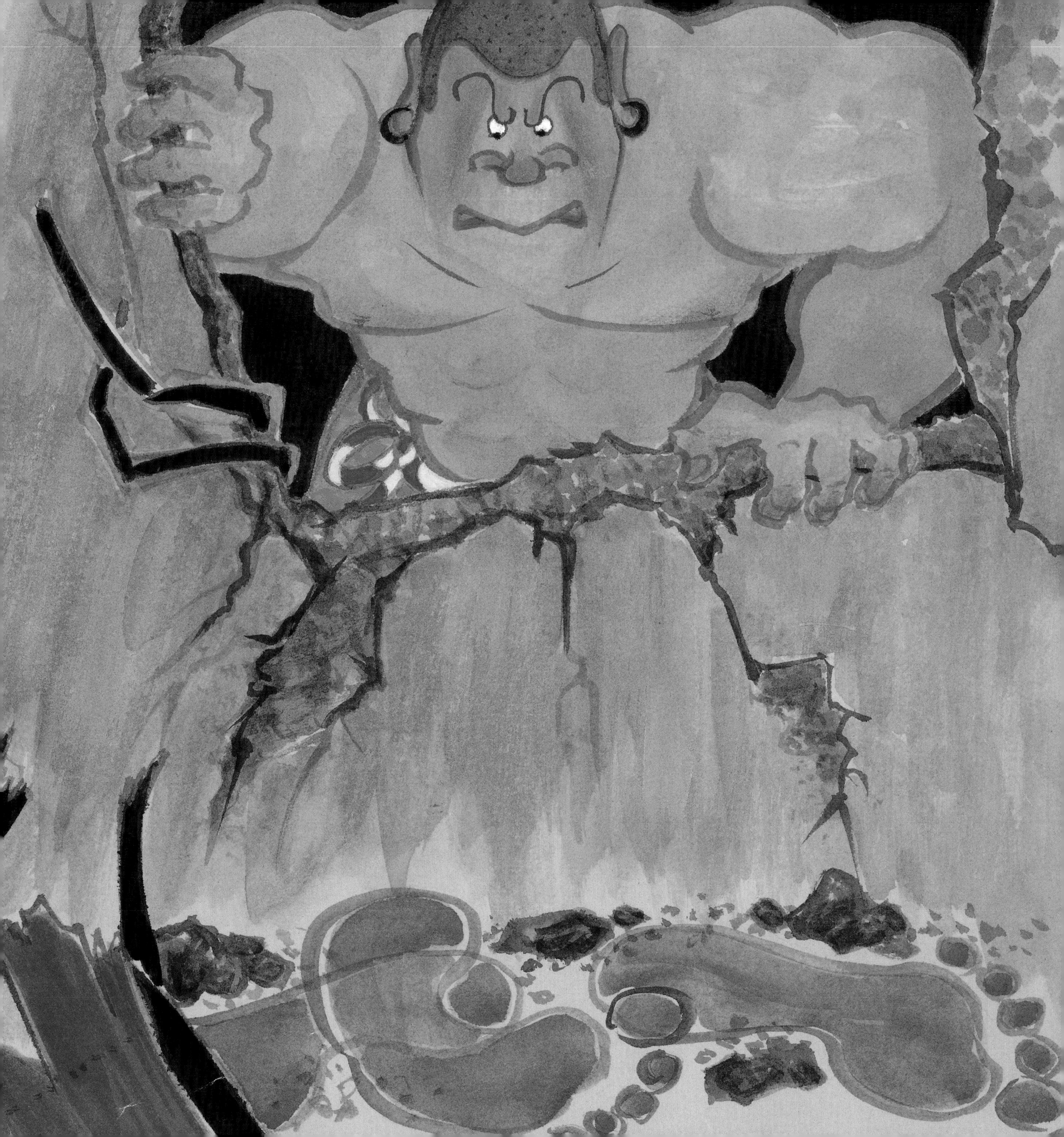

Dokkoi grabbed an anchor and ran after him. He followed the footprints down to the shore, but Ni-ou's boat was already disappearing over the horizon.

"Hey, Ni-ou!" Dokkoi boomed. "Are you going to run off home without challenging me?"

And he heaved the anchor at Ni-ou's boat.

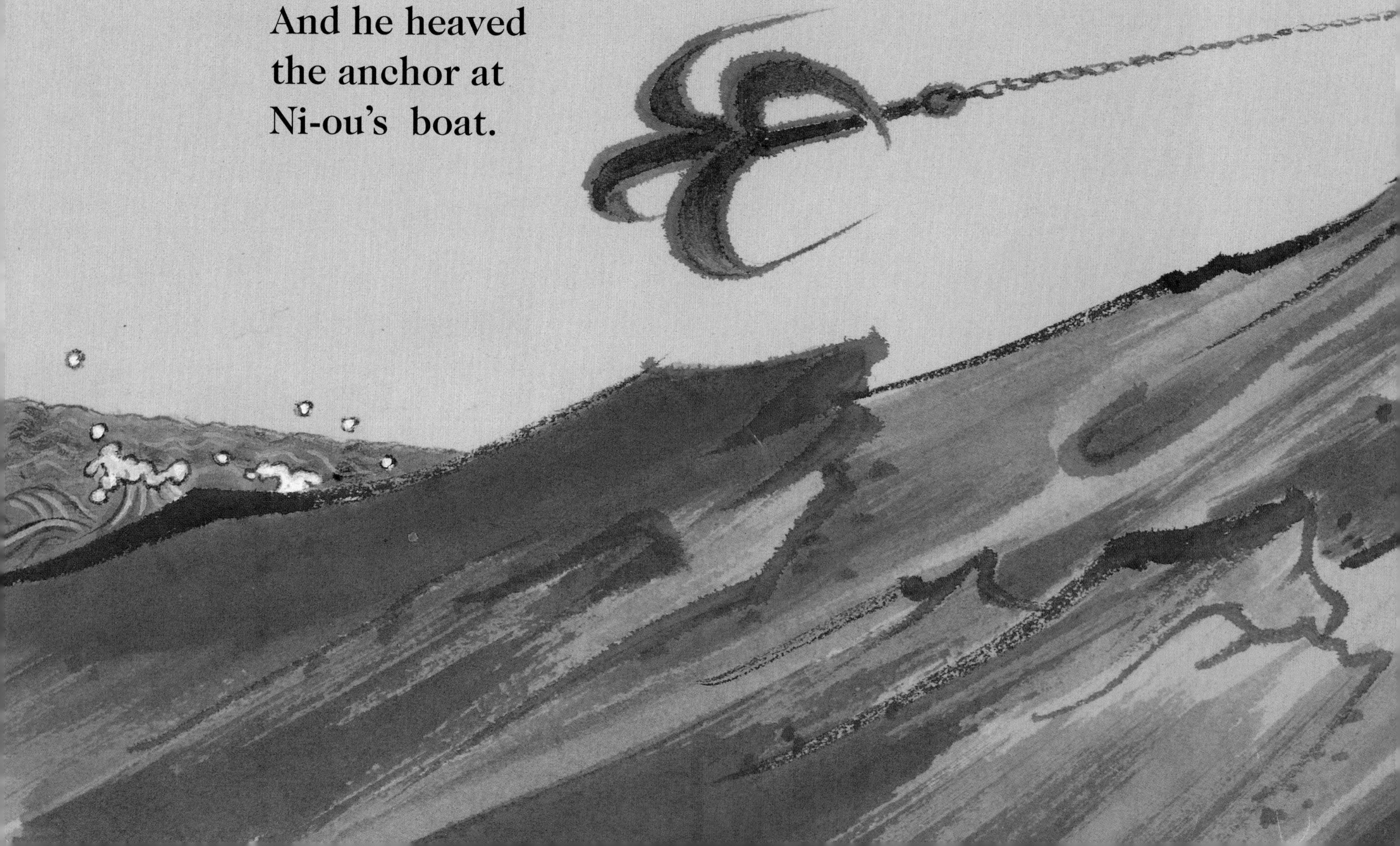

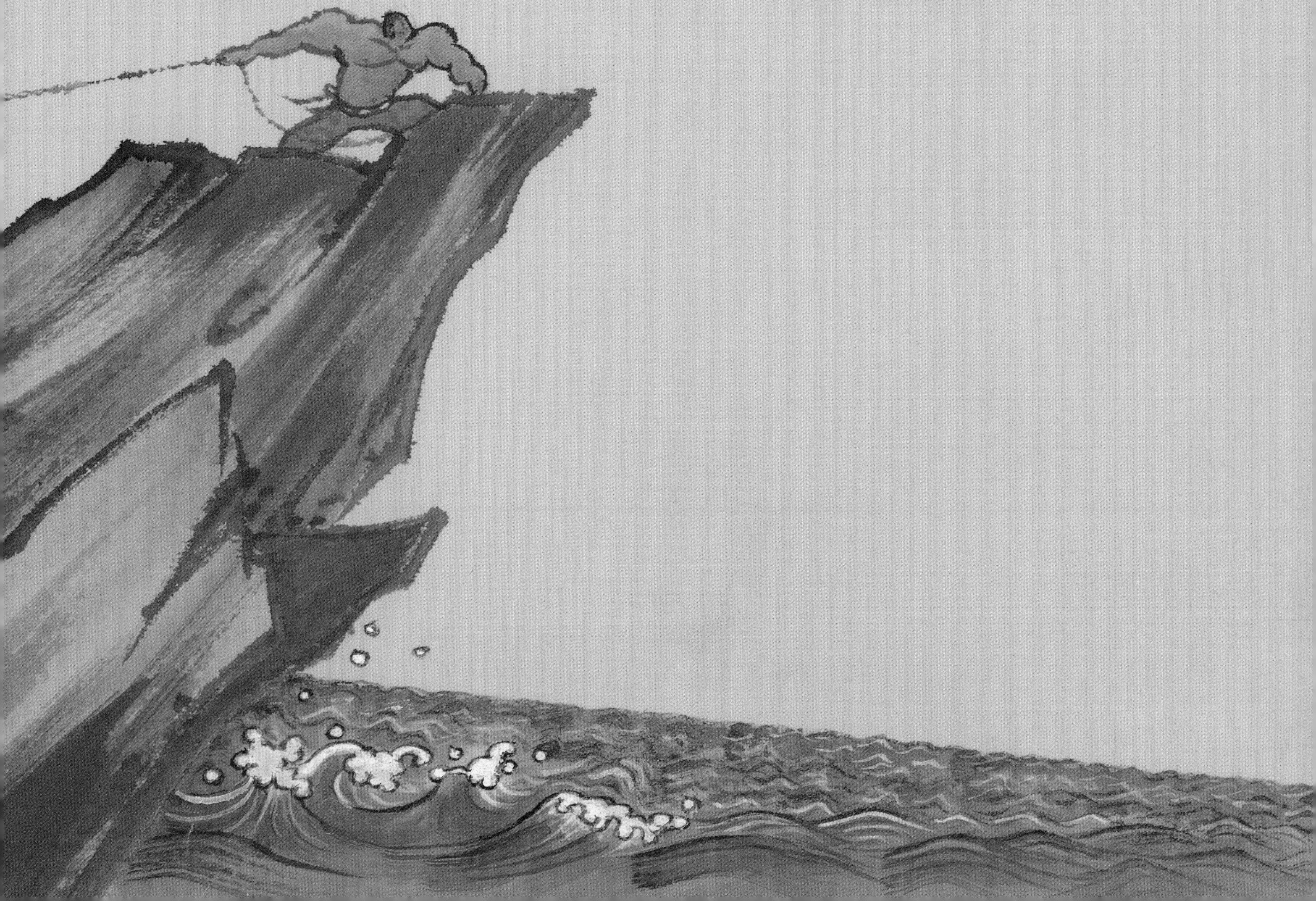

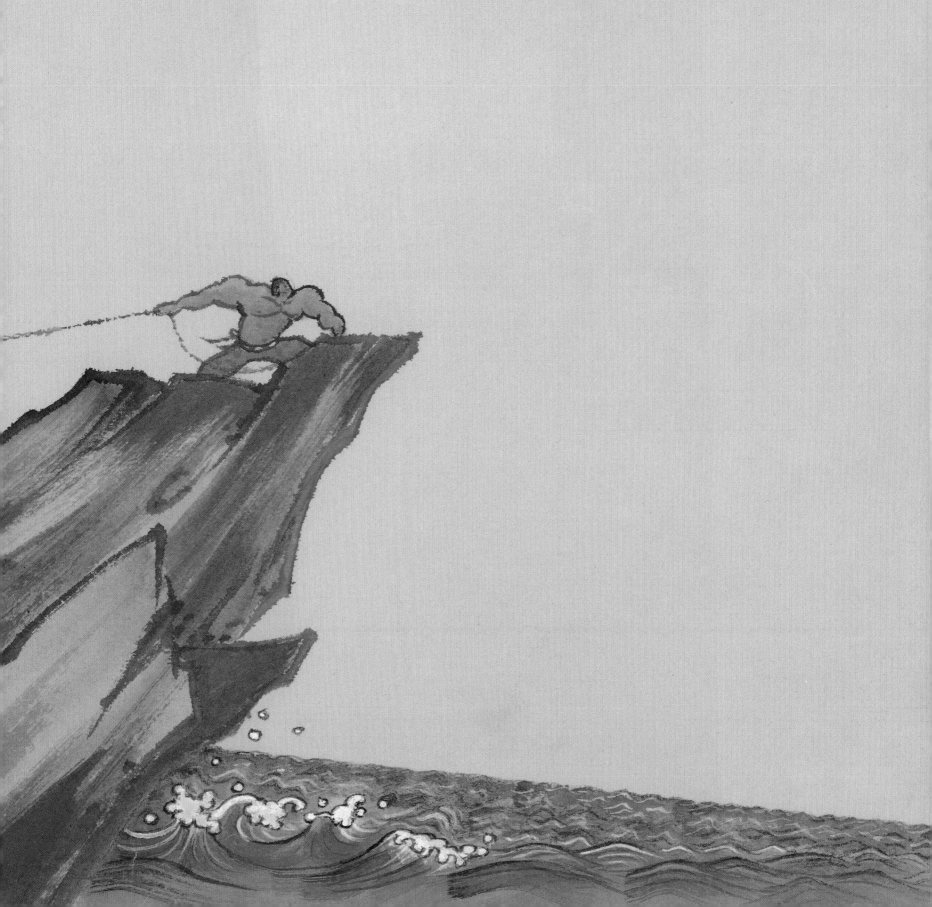

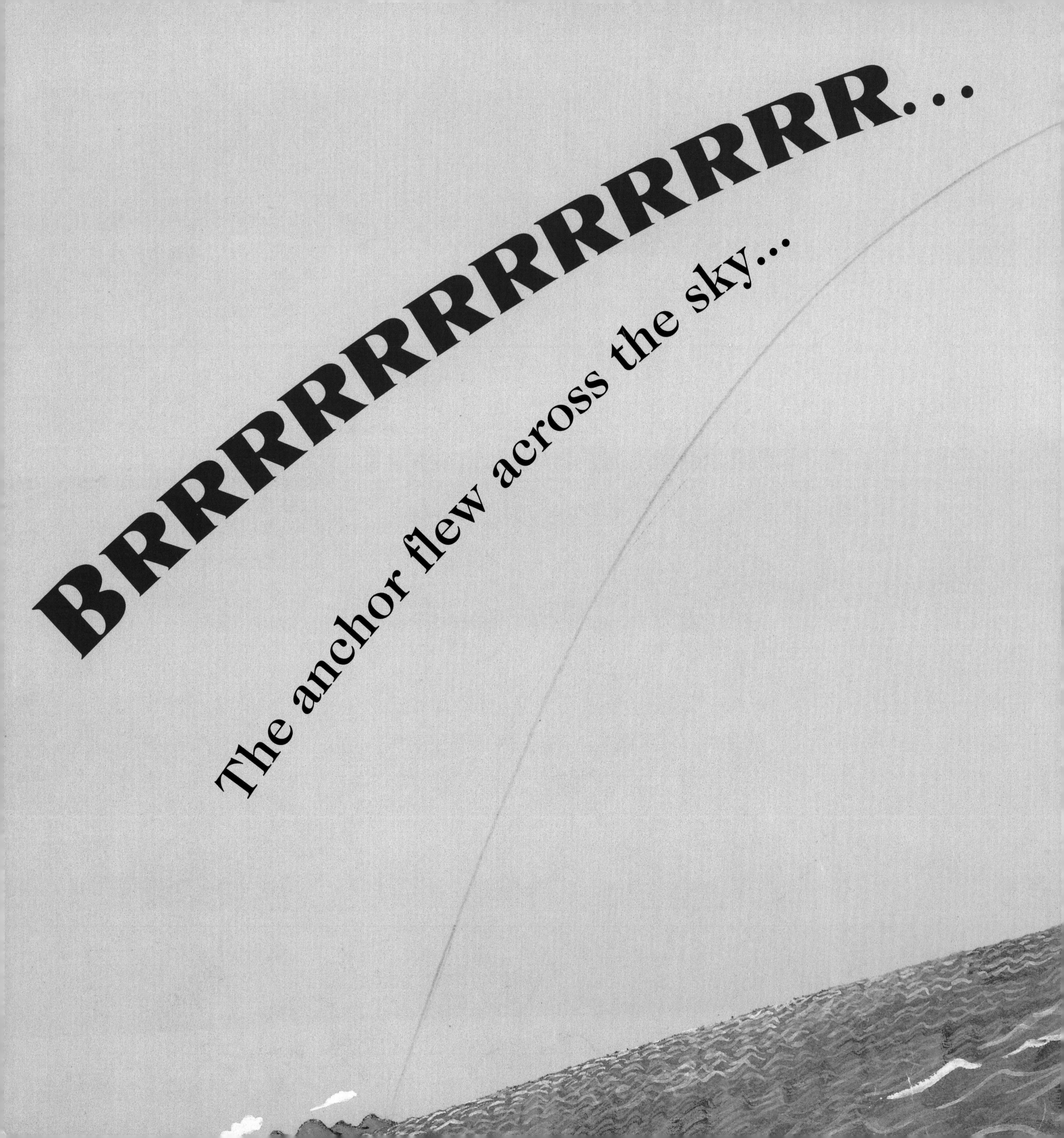

BRRRRRRRRRRRRR...

The anchor flew across the sky...

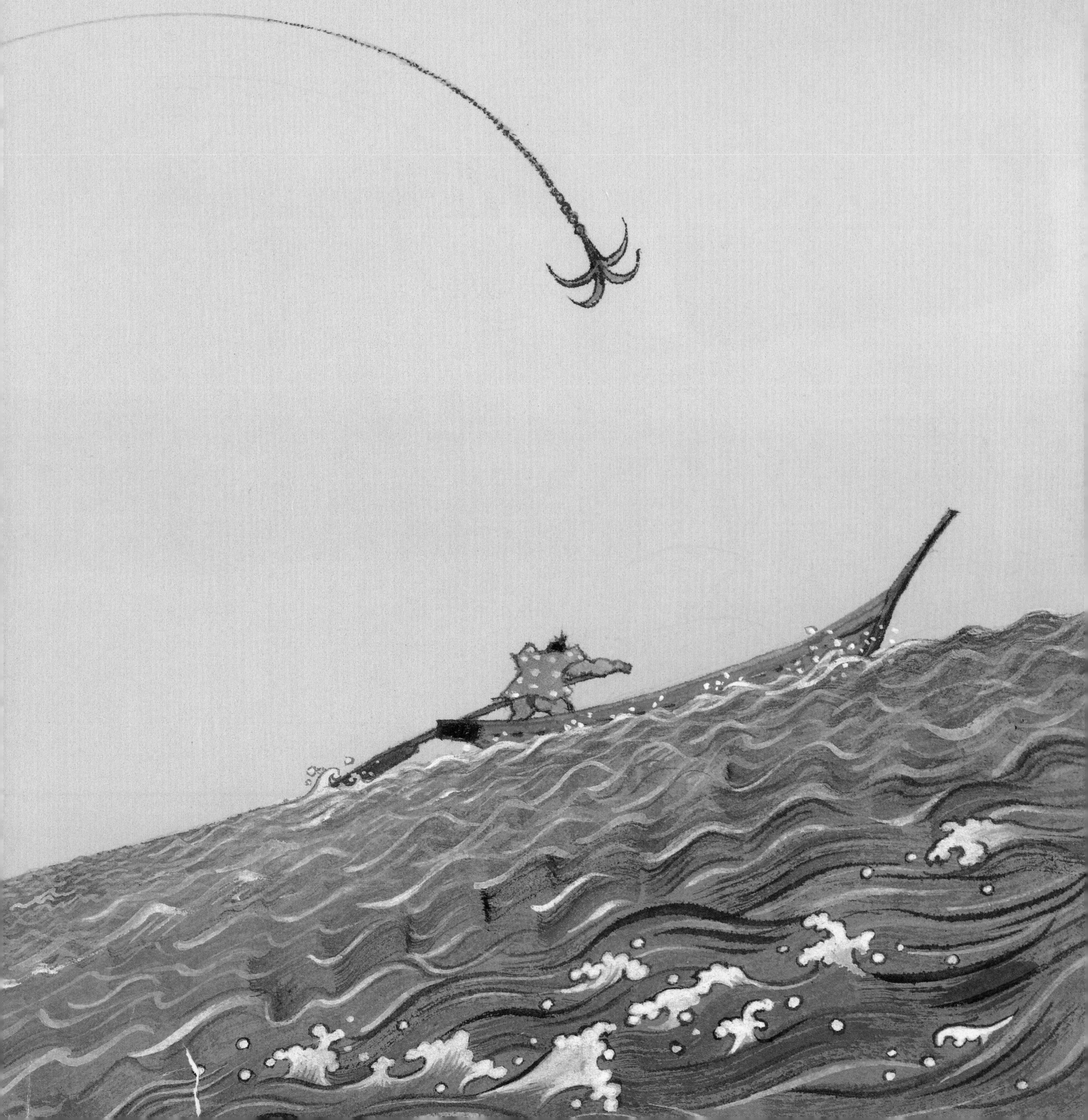

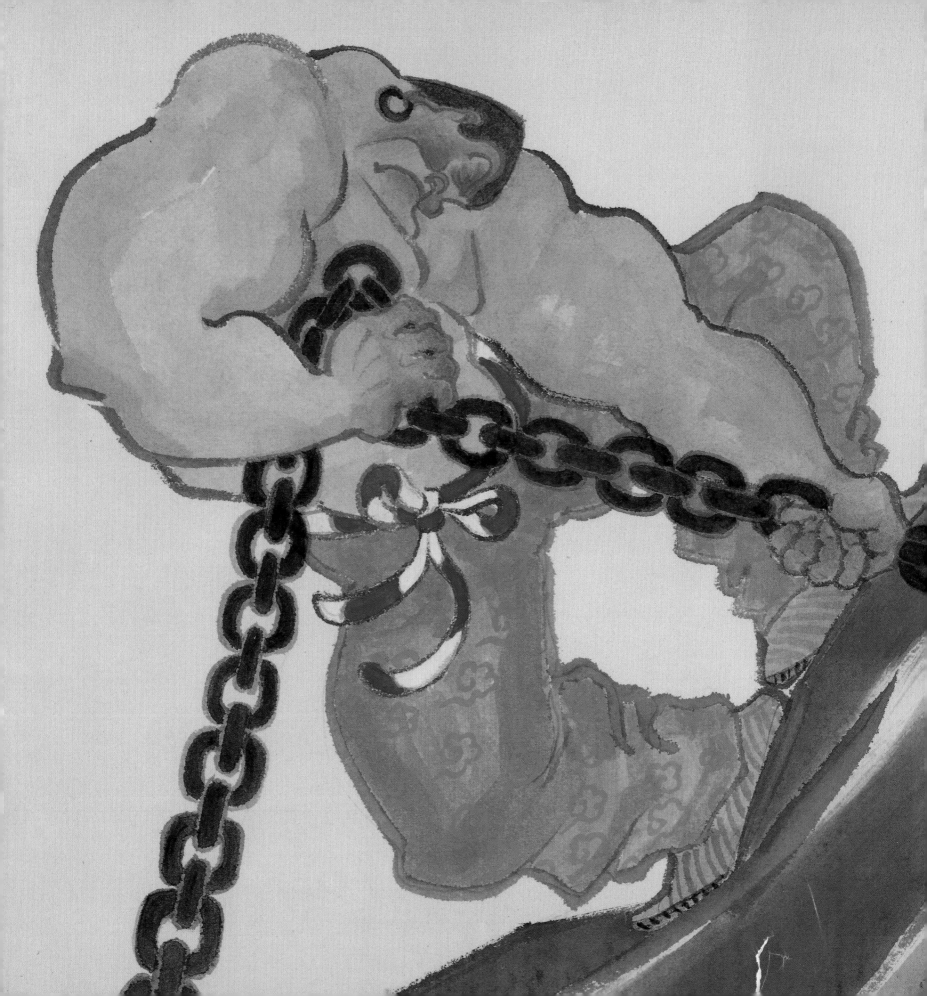

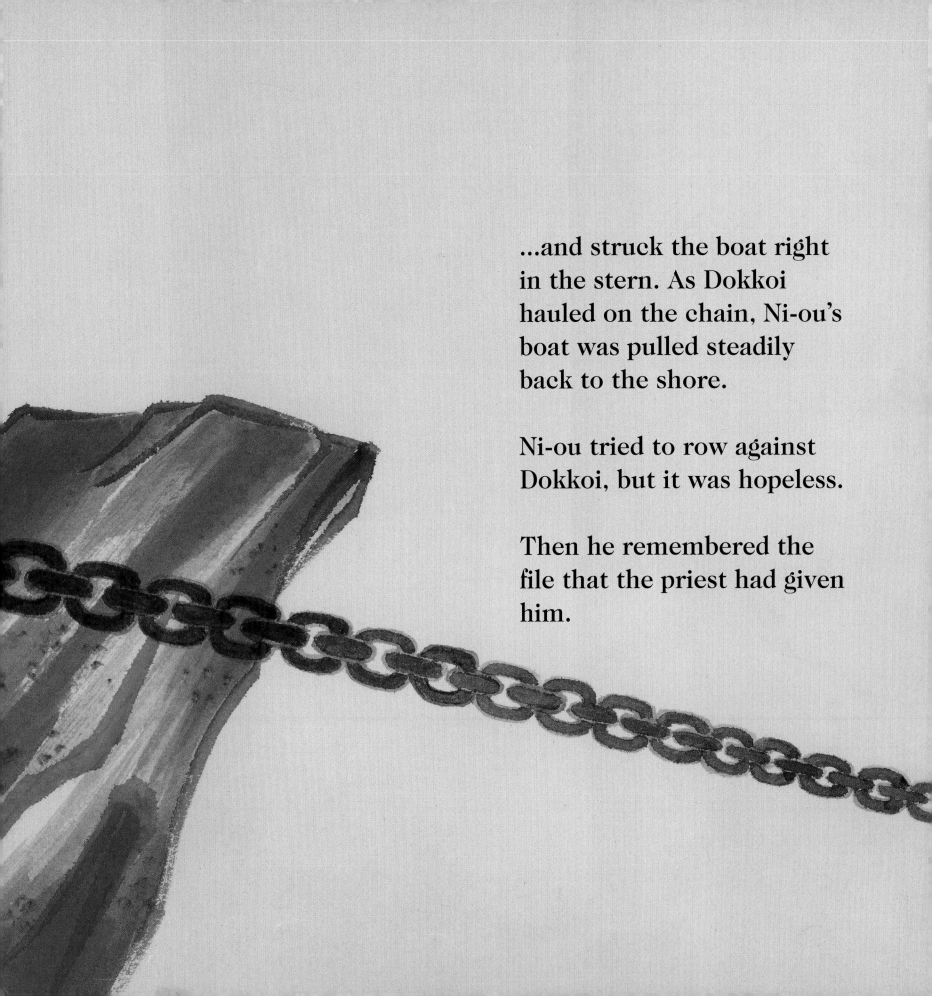

...and struck the boat right in the stern. As Dokkoi hauled on the chain, Ni-ou's boat was pulled steadily back to the shore.

Ni-ou tried to row against Dokkoi, but it was hopeless.

Then he remembered the file that the priest had given him.

He started rasping away at the chain.

Once, twice, three times...
and on the eighth try, Ni-ou finally
did it.

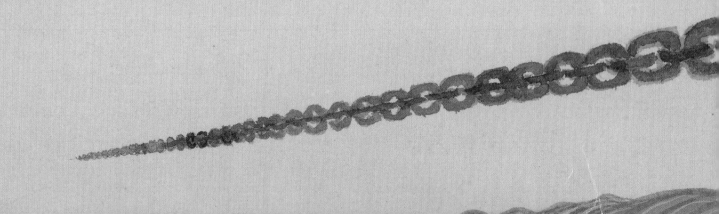

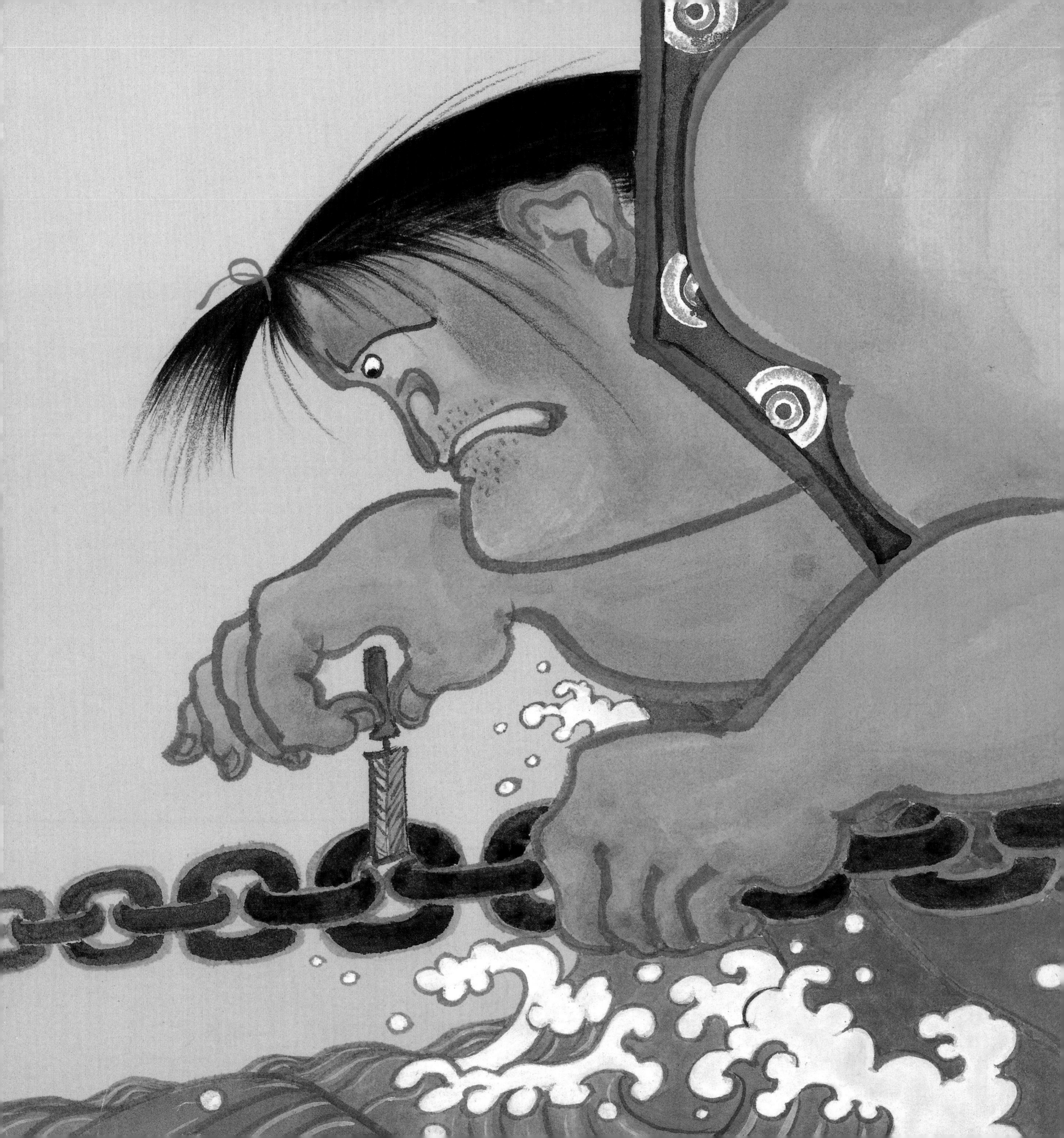

Dokkoi lost his balance
and down he fell.

The earth shook and
shook, and created an
enormous tidal wave
that carried Ni-ou all
the way to Japan.

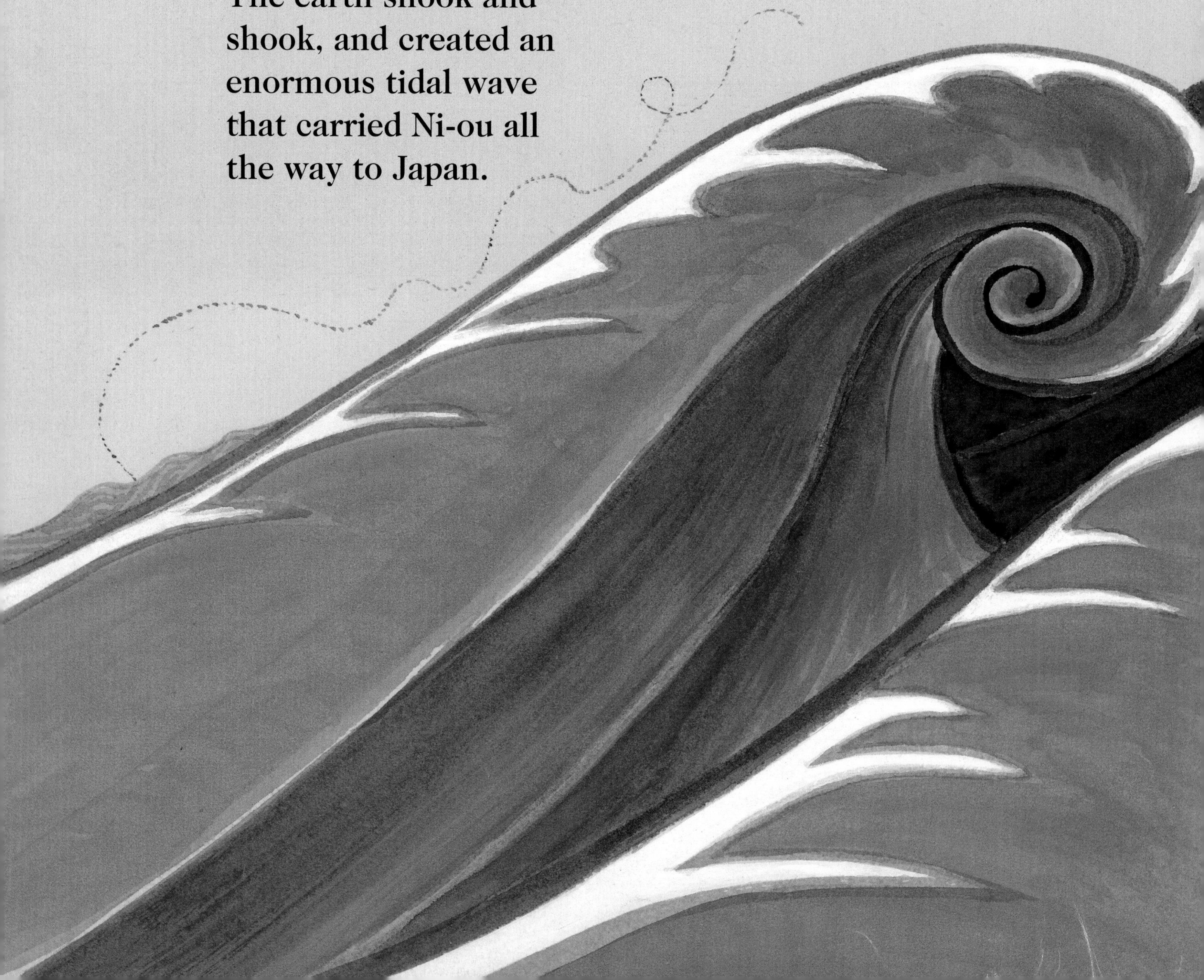

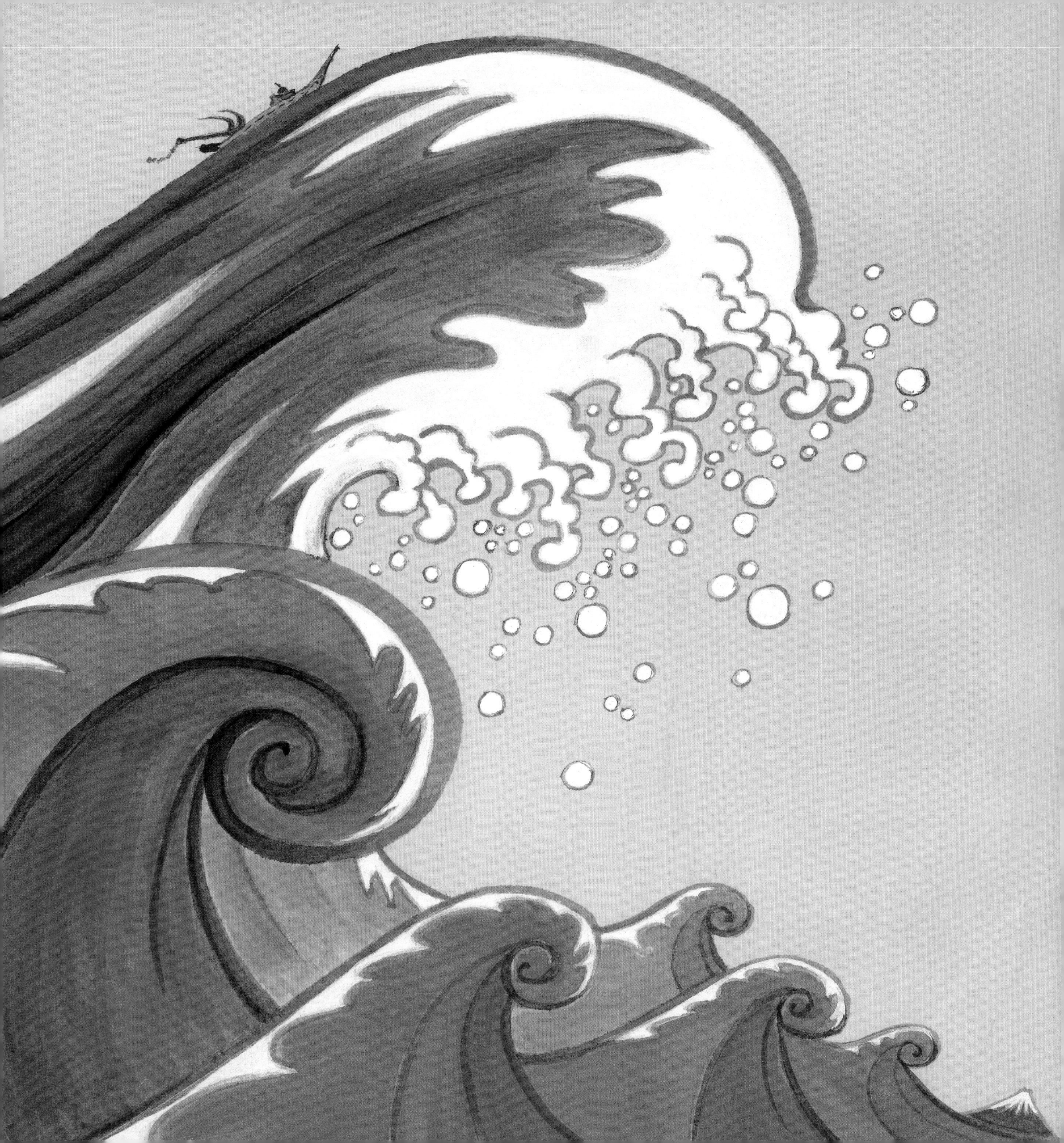

Back in China, Dokkoi looked around and sighed with relief. "Whoa!" he said. "How amazing to see him rip that chain apart—it's lucky I didn't fight *him!*"

And in Japan, Ni-ou was impressed too. “That was *so* close!” he said. “Dokkoi is enormous. He’s an incredibly powerful man!”

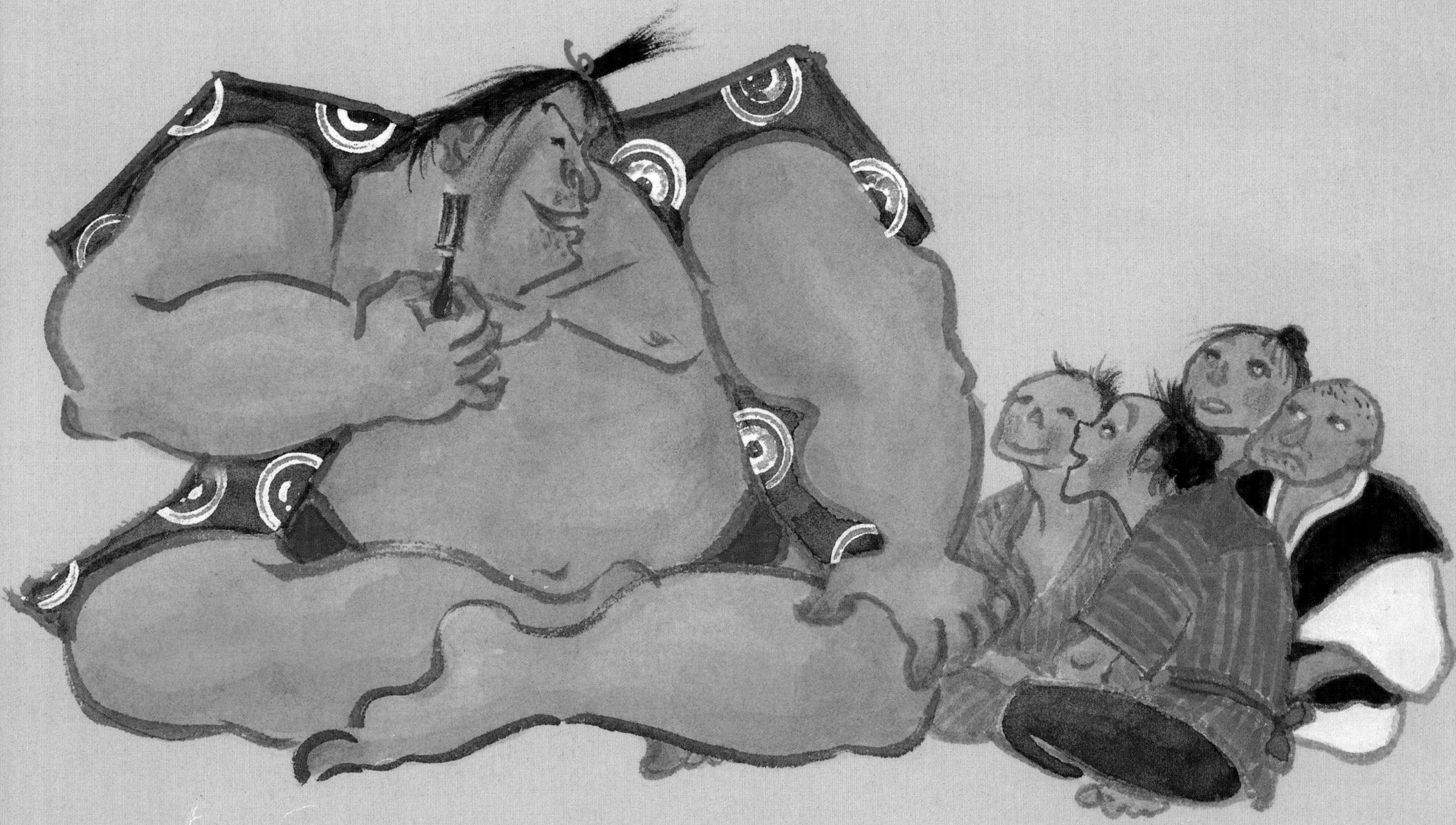

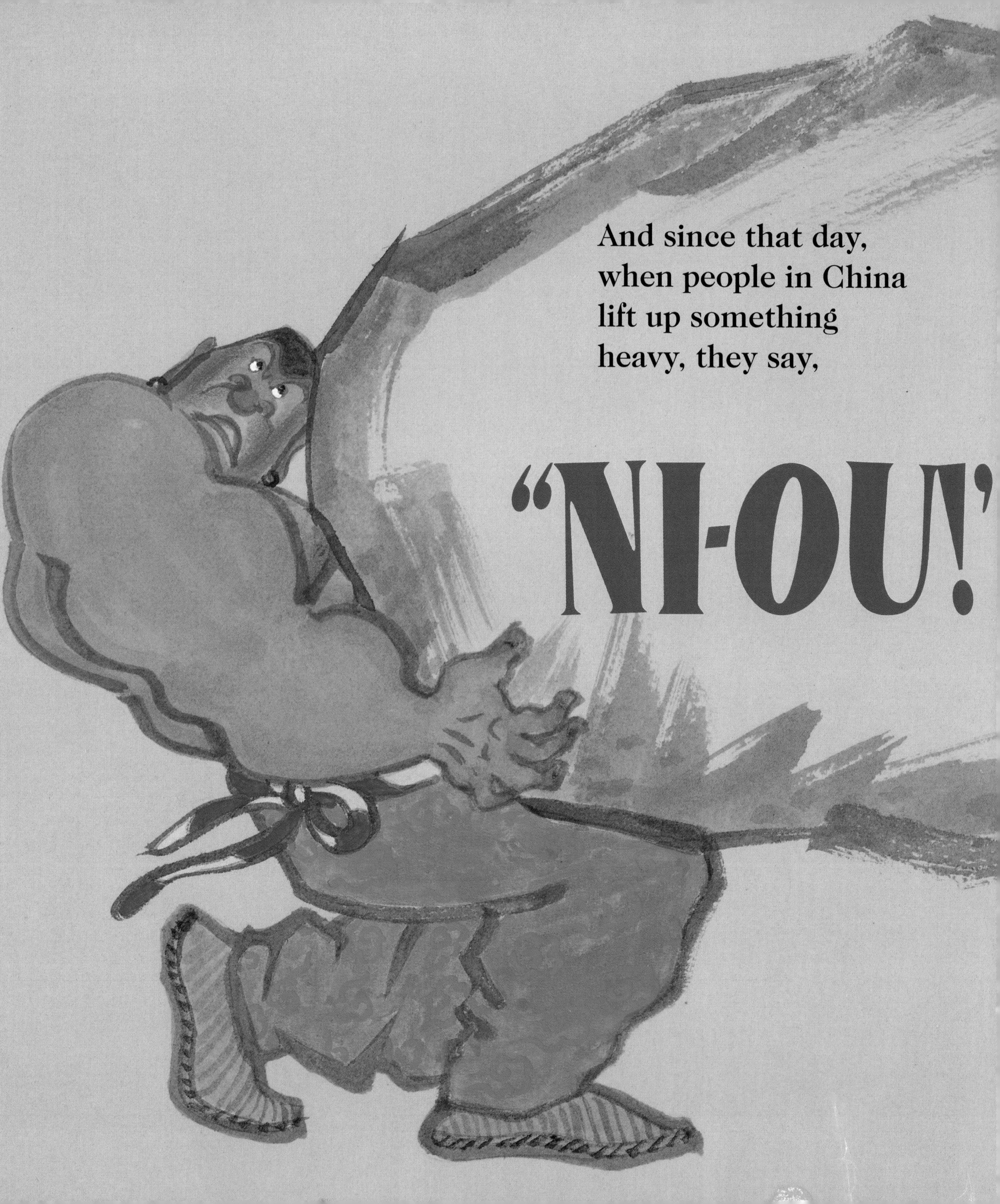

And since that day,
when people in China
lift up something
heavy, they say,

"NI-OU!"

and people in Japan
say,

"DOKKOI-SHO!"

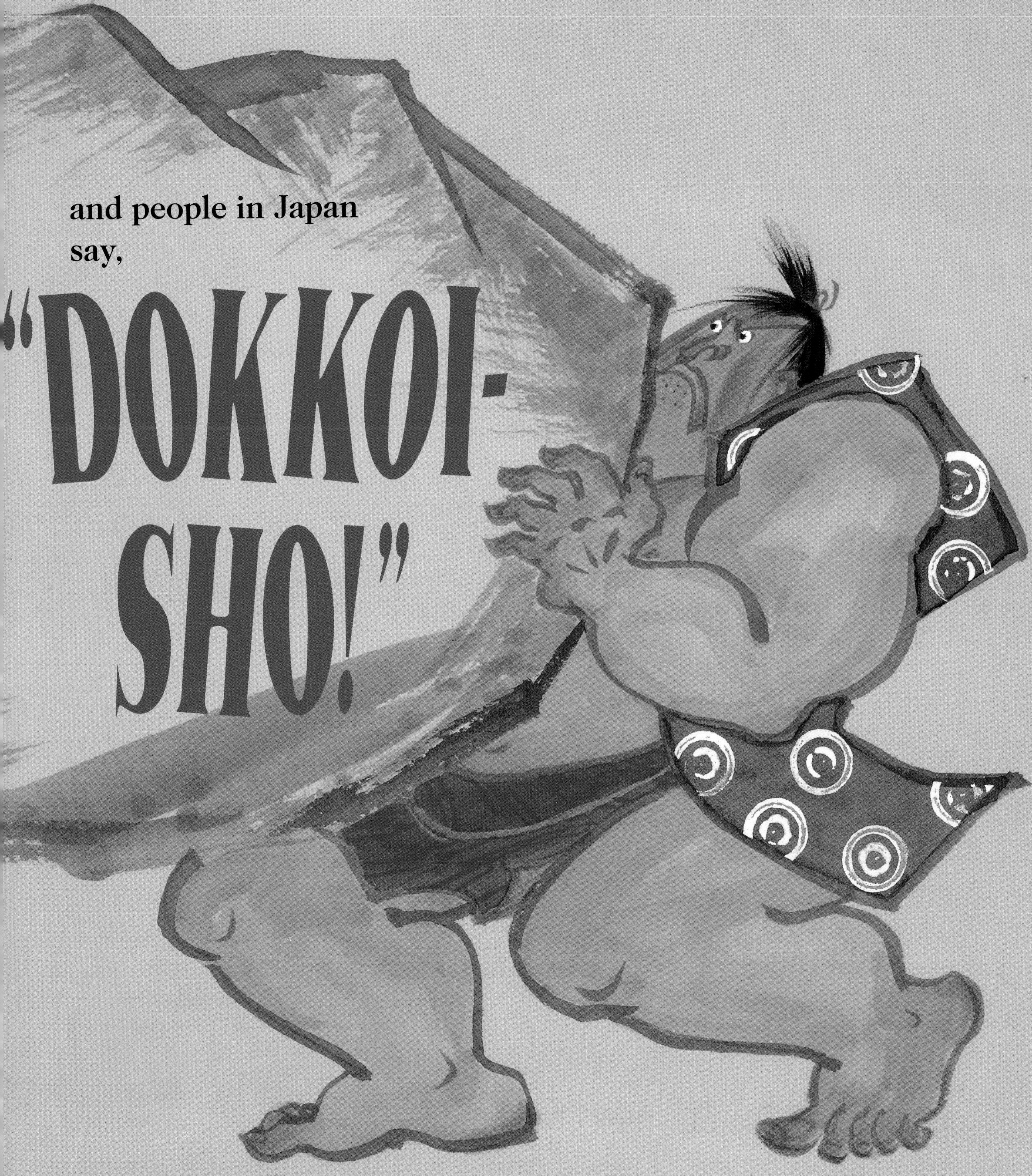

And Ni-ou started standing guard by Hachiman's temple gate in thanks for the priest's gift.

Copyright © 1997 by Junko Morimoto

Translated from an original Japanese story by Isao Morimoto

All rights reserved. No part of this book may be reproduced or transmitted in any form or by any means, electronic or mechanical, including photocopying, recording, or by any information storage and retrieval system, without permission in writing from the publisher.

Published by Crown Publishers, Inc., a Random House company, 201 East 50th Street, New York, New York 10022. Originally published in Australia as *The Two Bullies* by Junko Morimoto. This edition published by arrangement with Random House Australia through International Horizons Pty Ltd.

CROWN is a trademark of Crown Publishers, Inc.

www.randomhouse.com/kids

Library of Congress Cataloging-in-Publication Data
Morimoto, Junko.
The two bullies / Junko Morimoto ; translated from an original Japanese story by Isao Morimoto.
p. cm.
Summary: Two bullies, one from China and one from Japan, inadvertently intimidate one another before meeting face to face and never fight as a result.
[1. Bullies—Fiction. 2. China—Fiction. 3. Japan—Fiction] I. Morimoto, Isao. II. Title.
PZ7.M826747Tw   1999
[E]—dc21   98-41774

ISBN   0-517-80061-6 (trade)
ISBN   0-517-80062-4 (lib. bdg.)

Printed in Hong Kong

10 9 8 7 6 5 4 3 2 1

First American Edition

ROWE CHILDREN'S LIBRARY
LEDDING LIBRARY OF MILWAUKIE
10660 S.E. 21ST AVENUE
MILWAUKIE, OR 97222